THE USBORNE YOUNG SCIENTIST
JETS

**SEPECAT
Jaguar GR.1A
1972**

Lockheed L-1011 TriStar

Birdproof
windscreen

Weather
radar

Flight deck

Forward
entry
door

Fuselage

Fin

Engine air intakes

Rudder

Starboard wing

Port wing

Nose undercarriage

Main undercarriage

Tailplane

Engine pod

Flaps

Elevator

**Fairchild Republic
A-10A Thunderbolt II**

Credits

Written by
Mark Hewish
Revised text by
Christopher Cooper
Art and editorial direction
David Jefferis
Revised edition designed by
Paul Greenleaf
Text editor
Tony Allan
Educational adviser
Frank Blackwell
Revised by Alan Wright

Illustrators
Derek Bunce, Gordon Davies, Malcolm
English, Phil Green, Terry Hadler, John
Hutchinson and Michael Roffe
Copyright © 1991, 1982, 1976 Usborne
Publishing Ltd. Revised edition
published 1991

Acknowledgements
We wish to thank the following individuals and
organizations for their assistance and for
making available material in their collections.
Margaret Chester, Flight International,
Lufthansa Airlines; Neil Thomson, Rolls-
Royce Ltd, British Airways; L.F.E. Coombs,
McDonnell Douglas Corporation; Smiths
Industries; Airbus Industrie

First published in 1976. Revised and
updated 1982, 1991.
Usborne Publishing Ltd, Usborne House,
83-85 Saffron Hill, London EC1N 8RT,
England

The name Usborne and the device 🐝 are
Trade Marks of Usborne Publishing Ltd

Printed in Italy

On the cover: F16 'strike'
Falcon.
On this page: a flight of
Mirage F.1Cs

The experiments

Here is a checklist of the equipment you will need for the
experiments and things to do included in this book.

General equipment

Notebook and pencil
Ruler or tape-measure
Sticky tape★
Glue
Scissors
Watch (preferably with a second hand)
Rubber bands

For special experiments

Action and reaction (p.5): Balloon

**Air compression (p.6): Plastic detergent bottle
Modelling clay**

**Glider (p.8): Drinking straw
Sheet of stiff paper at least 22.5 cm. long**

Aerodynamic lift (p.9): Sheet of paper, roughly 15 x 20 cm.

Wing section (p.11): Three sheets of A4 paper (21 x 29.8 cm.)

**Artificial horizon (p.13): Plastic pot (an empty cream carton is ideal)
Match with sharpened end**

**Sound power (p.19): Wide-necked glass bottle
Sheet of polythene
Sugar**
★Cellophane tape

Weights and Measures

All the weights and measures used in this book are metric.
This list gives some equivalents in imperial measures.

mm. = millimetre
(1 inch = 25.4 mm.)

cm. = centimetre
(1 inch = 2.54 cm.)

m. = metre
(1 yard = 0.91 m.)

km. = kilometre
(1 mile = 1.6 km.)

k.p.h. = kilometres per hour
(1,000 m.p.h. = 1,609 k.p.h.)

sq. cm. = square centimetre
(1 square inch = 6.45 sq. cm.)

sq. m. = square metre
(1 square yard = 0.84 sq. m.)

A hectare is 10,000 sq. m.
(1 acre = 0.40 hectares)

kg. = kilogram
(1 stone = 6.35 kg.)

A tonne is 1,000 kg.
(1 ton = 1.02 tonnes)

1 litre is 1.76 pints

°C = degrees Centigrade
(Water freezes at 0°C and boils
at 100°C)

Contents

About this book

How do jet engines work? Why is there a bang when planes travel faster than sound? Why do jets leave vapour trails? Why do some planes have swing-wings?

Jets sets out to answer questions like these. It tells the story of the jet plane, from the beginnings in the 1930s to designs that are still on the drawing-board today. It explains the basic principles of jet flight. It describes what the most important instruments in an airliner cockpit are for, and how air traffic control works. It also covers such developments as supersonic airliners and vertical take-off, and the problems of noise pollution and jet-lag.

Jets also contains many safe and simple experiments that can be done at home with ordinary household equipment. They range from simple illustrations of scientific principles to projects like building a drinking-straw glider.

The first jets

It took a surprisingly long time for the jet engine to be invented, considering that the principle on which it works was known in ancient Greece. An inventor called Hero devised a sphere that was turned by escaping steam (see 1 below).

The idea of jet-propelled aircraft was first suggested in 1865, but the earliest planes to be built and flown were propellor-driven. Jet propulsion was not seriously considered again until 25 years after the Wright Brothers' first flight, when an English airman called Frank Whittle took up the idea.

In 1939 Germany's Heinkel He 178 became the first jet plane to fly.

The Italian Caproni-Campini, built in 1940, made the first cross-country flight.

1 Hero's steam sphere

▲ Pabst von Ohain, a German physicist, designed the engine for the world's first jet plane.
    After taking a degree at Göttingen University in Germany, he began building working models of gas turbines. In 1936 he was

2

employed by the aircraft manufacturer Ernst Heinkel.
    A year later he successfully tested his first jet engine. An improved version of it was installed in the specially designed He 178 test plane in 1939.

3

▲ Soon after dawn on August 27, 1939, Captain Erich Warsitz lifted the He 178 off the runway at the test base at Marienhe. He circled the airfield, then sideslipped in to land, completing the first jet flight ever.

6

7

8

▲ On May 15, 1941, the E.28/39 took to the air for the first time, flown by Flt. Lt. P. E. G. Sayer. Whittle's engine gave the Squirt, on its first flight, a performance almost as fast as a Spitfire's, and it later reached 750 k.p.h.

▲ The V-1 flying bomb was an offshoot of the development of the jet engine. It was powered by a pulse jet that allowed 'gulps' of air to pass into the combustion chamber, where they were mixed with petrol and ignited.

▲ Heinkel's experience with the 178 led to the wood-framed He 162 Salamander jet fighter. It first flew in December 1944. Only 116 were built, though plans were made to build 4,000 a month. Few Salamanders flew in combat.

Britain's Gloster E.28/39 was the brainchild of Frank Whittle, who had worked for 12 years on jet engine development before its maiden flight in 1941.

The Bell XP-59A Airacomet brought the U.S. into the jet age in 1942. Its twin turbojet engines were developed from Whittle's designs.

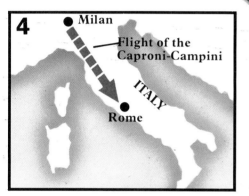

4

Milan

Flight of the Caproni-Campini

ITALY

Rome

▲ The Caproni-Campini made its maiden flight exactly a year after the He 178. In 1941 it flew from Milan to Rome, a distance of 470 km. It was a slow flyer, though, with a top speed of only 375 k.p.h.

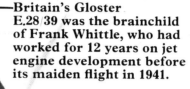

5

▲ Frank Whittle began thinking about jet propulsion in the late 1920s, when he was at the Royal Air Force College, Cranwell.

The Air Ministry rejected his designs, but in 1935 a friend raised the money to back his work, and Power Jets Ltd. was formed.

Their first working engine ran on April 12, 1937, and in July 1939 the company was awarded a contract to build an engine for the experimental Gloster E.28/39 – nicknamed the Squirt.

9

British Meteor

German Me 262

▲ The Me 262 and Meteor twin-engined warplanes both went into service in World War 2, but they never fought one another. The Me 262 had swept wings – a development pioneered by German aircraft designers.

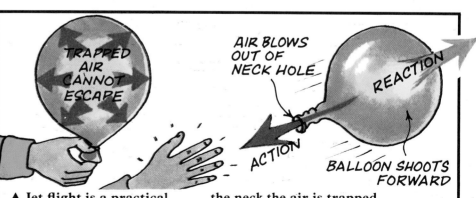

TRAPPED AIR CANNOT ESCAPE

AIR BLOWS OUT OF NECK HOLE

REACTION

ACTION

BALLOON SHOOTS FORWARD

▲ Jet flight is a practical application of the Third Law of Motion, which states that for every action there is an equal and opposite reaction. Try it for yourself by blowing up a balloon. While you hold the neck the air is trapped, but when you let go it rushes out. This action causes a reaction, so the balloon shoots forward in the opposite direction to the air. Jet planes speed along in a similar way.

Turbojet and turbofan

Early jet engines were pure turbojets. Air passing through them goes through four main stages. First it is sucked in through the intake. Then it is compressed. The compressed air is mixed with fuel and set alight. Finally the hot gases produced are forced back through the exhaust, driving the aircraft forward.

Some jets now use large fans to draw in more air. This kind of engine is called a turbofan.

Turbojet-powered Concorde

The turbojet shown opposite is the Rolls-Royce Olympus engine used in Concordes. Air entering the intake (1) passes through the compressor (2) – a series of vanes that pack it densely together. It is mixed with vaporized kerosene in the combustion chamber (3) and burned.

The hot gases this produces roar through the turbine (4), which spins round like windmill blades in wind, turning the vanes in the compressor as it goes. They then pass through a nozzle (5) into the afterburner (6), where more fuel is burned to provide extra thrust.

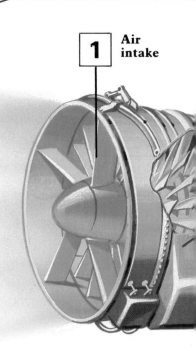

1 Air intake

1 Air compression

Jet engines have compressors to pack as much air as possible into the combustion chamber. The amount of thrust an engine gives increases as more fuel is used, and the fuel needs oxygen in the air to make it burn — so the thrust depends also on the amount of air that is sucked in.

Cold air is best, as it is denser than hot air. But air heats up as it is compressed. Try pumping up a bicycle tyre. You will soon find that compression and friction combined have warmed pump and tyre up.

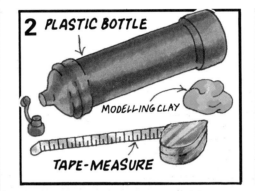

2 PLASTIC BOTTLE
MODELLING CLAY
TAPE-MEASURE

▲ This is a neat and simple experiment which shows just how powerful a force compressed air can exert. All you need is an empty plastic detergent bottle, a piece of modelling clay, and a tape-measure.

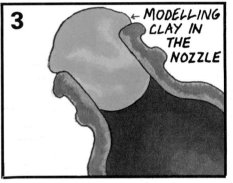

3 ← MODELLING CLAY IN THE NOZZLE

▲ Take the nozzle off the bottle, and ease a lump of modelling clay into the neck. Make sure the seal is airtight by squeezing the bottle gently and listening for air leaks. Take the bottle outside or into a large room.

4

▲ Lay the bottle on the ground, then jump on it! The pressure of compressed air will blow the modelling clay cork up to 20 m away. Mark the spot where it lands, then see which of your friends can make it go furthest.

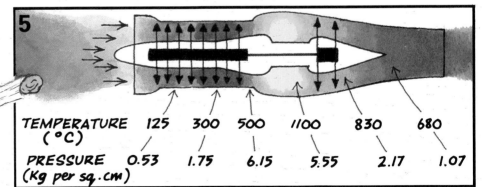

5

TEMPERATURE (°C)	125	300	500	1100	830	680
PRESSURE (Kg per sq. cm)	0.53	1.75	6.15	5.55	2.17	1.07

▲ This diagram shows what happens to the temperature and pressure of air as it passes through the Olympus turbojet of a Concorde flying at twice the speed of sound nearly 20,000 m up. The compressors increase the air pressure more than ten times, so that as much as possible is crammed into the combustion chamber. The air temperature, which has steadily increased in the compressor, is doubled when the fuel ignites, while the pressure starts to fall.

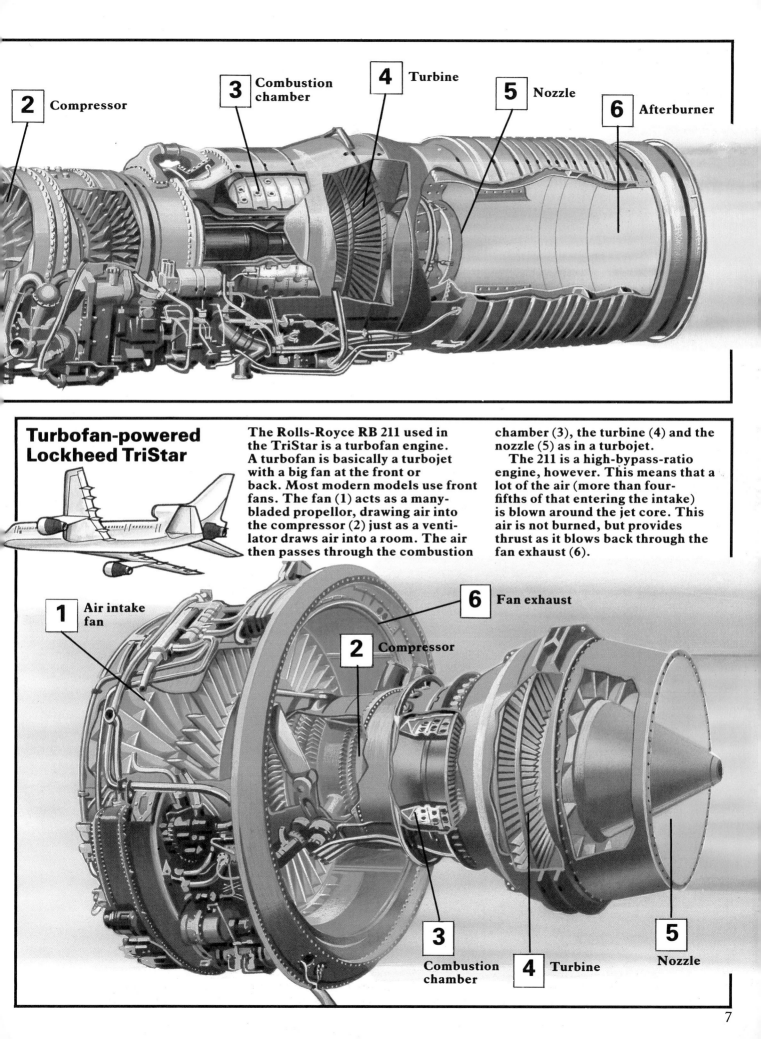

2 Compressor

3 Combustion chamber

4 Turbine

5 Nozzle

6 Afterburner

Turbofan-powered Lockheed TriStar

The Rolls-Royce RB 211 used in the TriStar is a turbofan engine. A turbofan is basically a turbojet with a big fan at the front or back. Most modern models use front fans. The fan (1) acts as a many-bladed propellor, drawing air into the compressor (2) just as a ventilator draws air into a room. The air then passes through the combustion chamber (3), the turbine (4) and the nozzle (5) as in a turbojet.

The 211 is a high-bypass-ratio engine, however. This means that a lot of the air (more than four-fifths of that entering the intake) is blown around the jet core. This air is not burned, but provides thrust as it blows back through the fan exhaust (6).

1 Air intake fan

6 Fan exhaust

2 Compressor

3 Combustion chamber

4 Turbine

5 Nozzle

How and why jets fly

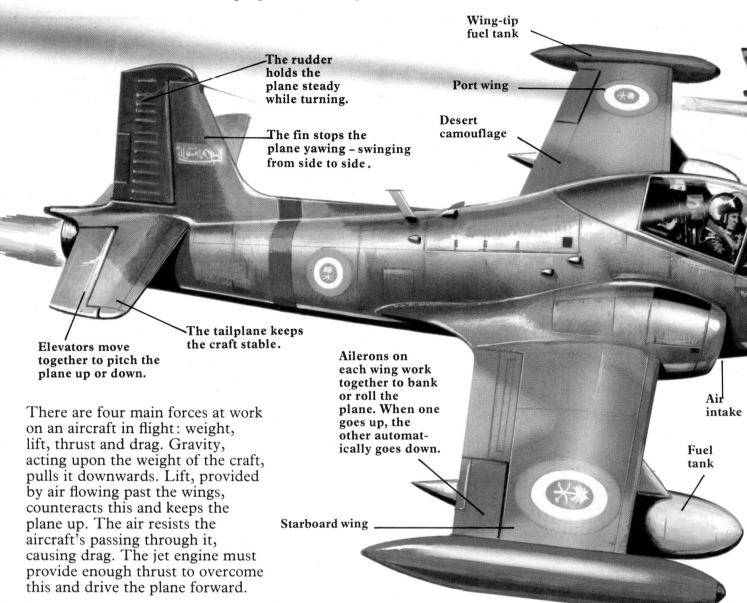

The rudder holds the plane steady while turning.

The fin stops the plane yawing – swinging from side to side.

Wing-tip fuel tank

Port wing

Desert camouflage

Elevators move together to pitch the plane up or down.

The tailplane keeps the craft stable.

Ailerons on each wing work together to bank or roll the plane. When one goes up, the other automatically goes down.

Air intake

Fuel tank

Starboard wing

There are four main forces at work on an aircraft in flight: weight, lift, thrust and drag. Gravity, acting upon the weight of the craft, pulls it downwards. Lift, provided by air flowing past the wings, counteracts this and keeps the plane up. The air resists the aircraft's passing through it, causing drag. The jet engine must provide enough thrust to overcome this and drive the plane forward.

How to make and flight-test your own aircraft

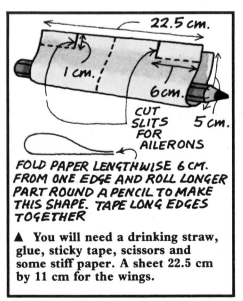

22.5 cm.

1 cm.

6 cm.

5 cm.

CUT SLITS FOR AILERONS

FOLD PAPER LENGTHWISE 6 CM. FROM ONE EDGE AND ROLL LONGER PART ROUND A PENCIL TO MAKE THIS SHAPE. TAPE LONG EDGES TOGETHER

▲ You will need a drinking straw, glue, sticky tape, scissors and some stiff paper. A sheet 22.5 cm by 11 cm for the wings.

18 cm.

FOLD DOTTED LINES

1 cm.

5 cm.

5 cm.

GLUE FIN

CUT SLITS FOR ELEVATORS

2.5 cm.

4 cm.

▲ Cut a piece of paper 20 cm by 3.5 cm for the tail. Cut and fold it as shown, making the rudder extend 1 cm beyond the tailplanes.

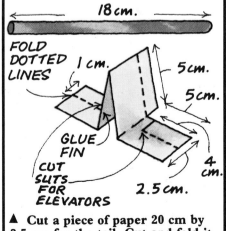

PAPER CLIPS

TAPE

3 cm.

TAPE

▲ Tape the wings and tail to the straw. Attach a paper-clip to the straw and test the glider. Go on attaching clips until the glider flies smoothly.

Elevon

1 LONG PENCIL
15 cm.
TAPE
10 cm.
(15 x 20 cm.)
SHEET

2 BLOW HARD
PAPER WING MOVES UPWARDS

Elevon

Wings shaped like triangles are called deltas after the Greek letter △ or delta. They are used on many high-speed planes. There is usually no tailplane on delta-winged planes, and the elevators and ailerons are combined to form elevons. The elevons move together to pitch the plane up or down, and in opposite directions for banking and rolling.

▲ To find out how lift works, take a thin sheet of paper, about 20 cm. by 15 cm., and fold it into a wing shape as shown. Tape the two loose edges together. Find a pencil more than 15 cm. long and slide it into the loop of paper.

▲ Hold the pencil so that the top edge of the 'wing' almost touches your lower lip. Now blow down over the outer surface. The wing will rise and remain level as long as you keep blowing. Your breath is acting like air over a plane wing.

Anti-glare panel painted in front of cockpit

The jet on the left is a British Aerospace (BAC) Strikemaster ground attack plane of the Saudi Arabian Air Force. The plane above is a Mirage fighter-bomber with French markings.

3 LOW AIR PRESSURE
HIGHER AIR PRESSURE

4 CROSS-SECTIONS OF DIFFERENT WINGS

▲ The upper surface of an aircraft wing is more curved than the lower surface, and air has to accelerate over the top to catch up with that flowing underneath. This 'stretches' the air on top, creating an area of low pressure that sucks the wing up.

▲ Wings, also known as aerofoils, have various shapes according to the sort of job they are designed for. They are usually thin on very fast planes, and may be flattened or wedge-shaped to increase lift under different conditions.

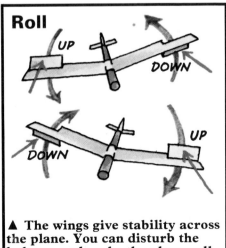
Roll
UP
DOWN
DOWN
UP

▲ The wings give stability across the plane. You can disturb the balance and make the plane roll by moving the ailerons as shown.

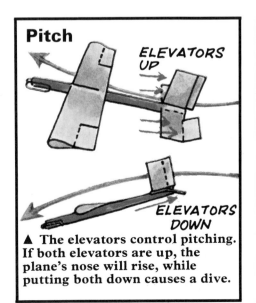
Pitch
ELEVATORS UP
ELEVATORS DOWN

▲ The elevators control pitching. If both elevators are up, the plane's nose will rise, while putting both down causes a dive.

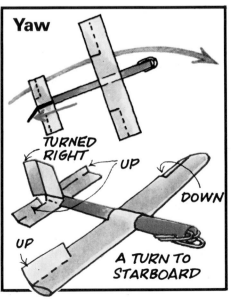
Yaw
TURNED RIGHT
UP
DOWN
UP
A TURN TO STARBOARD

Jet-Age airliners

The age of the pure-jet airliner dawned on May 2, 1952, when a Comet 1 owned by the British Overseas Airways Corporation made its first scheduled flight, from London to Johannesburg. Jet services halved flying times on long-distance trips. In 1959 Pan American World Airways started round-the-world flights with Boeing 707s. Nowadays almost all airliners are jet-powered.

The Airbus series of jetliners began service in 1974. Parts for these aircraft are made in several European countries and assembled at Toulouse in France.

1 Fuel tanks, two to each wing. Fuel can also be stored in the wing centre section.

2 Ram-air turbine drops down from the starboard wing root in case of emergency. A small propellor on the front rotates in the airflow and generates electrical power.

3 Wide-body cabin can seat more than 300 passengers. It is 5.65 m. across.

4 Fuselage is made of aluminium alloy - as are the tail and wings.

5 Flight deck for pilot, co-pilot and flight engineer.

6 Radome protects radar equipment, which detects clouds and rain.

7 General Electric CF6 engine, one under each wing. The CF6 is a turbofan giving 23,133 kg. of thrust.

8 Underfloor freight holds can carry pallets, containers or loose cargo.

9 Main undercarriage has four wheels on each leg.

10 Auxiliary power unit in the tail is a miniature jet engine providing electrical power, and compressed air for starting the engines and for air-conditioning.

The Comet crashes

▲ The de Havilland Comet 1 was a great success when it went into service in 1952. It halved journey times, carrying 36 passengers in comfort at nearly 800 k.p.h. well above the worst weather. For two years things went well.

▲ In January 1954, disaster struck. A Comet crashed into the sea after taking off from Rome, and all 35 people on board were killed. Flights were suspended for a time. When they resumed, a second Comet went down in flames, killing 17 people.

▲ All Comets were grounded. Royal Navy salvage vessels were sent to the scene of the first crash - the second plane had gone down in very deep water - and with the help of divers they recovered nearly two-thirds of the sunken plane.

Make a wing section

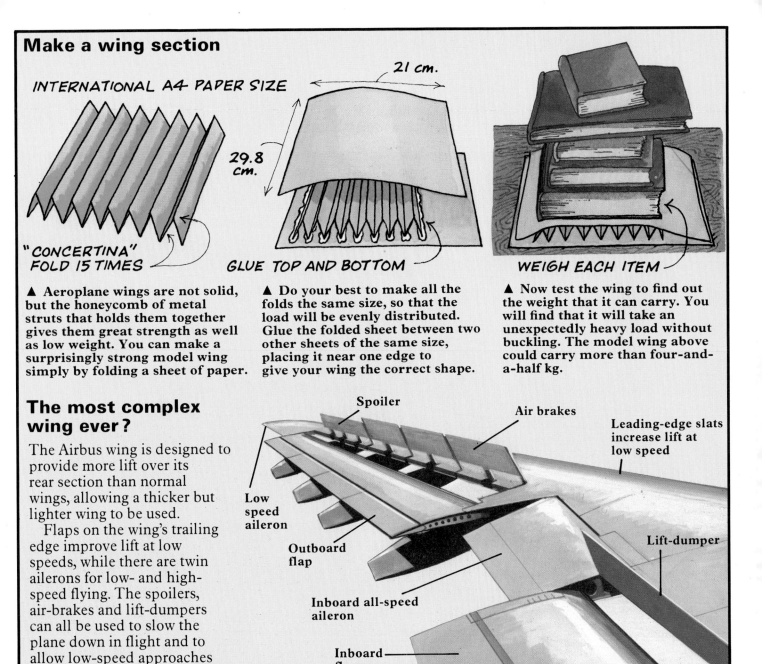

INTERNATIONAL A4 PAPER SIZE

"CONCERTINA" FOLD 15 TIMES

21 cm.

29.8 cm.

GLUE TOP AND BOTTOM

WEIGH EACH ITEM

▲ Aeroplane wings are not solid, but the honeycomb of metal struts that holds them together gives them great strength as well as low weight. You can make a surprisingly strong model wing simply by folding a sheet of paper.

▲ Do your best to make all the folds the same size, so that the load will be evenly distributed. Glue the folded sheet between two other sheets of the same size, placing it near one edge to give your wing the correct shape.

▲ Now test the wing to find out the weight that it can carry. You will find that it will take an unexpectedly heavy load without buckling. The model wing above could carry more than four-and-a-half kg.

The most complex wing ever?

The Airbus wing is designed to provide more lift over its rear section than normal wings, allowing a thicker but lighter wing to be used.

Flaps on the wing's trailing edge improve lift at low speeds, while there are twin ailerons for low- and high-speed flying. The spoilers, air-brakes and lift-dumpers can all be used to slow the plane down in flight and to allow low-speed approaches for landing.

Spoiler

Air brakes

Leading-edge slats increase lift at low speed

Low speed aileron

Outboard flap

Inboard all-speed aileron

Inboard flap

Lift-dumper

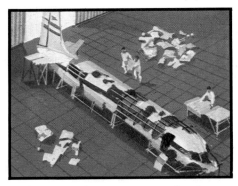

▲ The wreckage was sent back to Farnborough, England. It was reassembled on a frame the size and shape of a real Comet. Most of the fuselage, parts of the wings, and all four engines were found and wired into place.

▲ Another Comet was put in a tank, with its wings sticking out. Jacks bent the wings, while water was pumped into the fuselage to create strains equal to those of thousands of hours of flying. The fuselage eventually ripped apart.

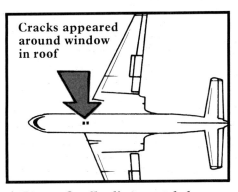

Cracks appeared around window in roof

▲ It was finally discovered that the crash had been caused by cracks spreading from a rivet hole, causing the pressurized cabin to explode. Jet design was altered as a result, and nowadays metal fatigue is kept under control.

Inside the cockpit

The A320 Airbus has an advanced computerized flight deck. There are two pilots, but no flight engineer is required to keep a watch on the aircraft's systems.

The controls

 Flight controls. Side-stick controllers replace the traditional joysticks. Large pedals control the rudder, elevators, etc.

Flight instruments. Computer displays show course, speed, height, position of radio beacons, cloud and rain ahead, etc.

 Aircraft systems displays. Fuel levels, flap positions, etc. are indicated — even if the cabin seat-belt signs are on.

Overhead panels. These carry controls and warning lights for the aircraft's fuel, electrical and hydraulic systems.

 Engine controls. Throttles control the power of each engine separately. Other levers control flaps, slats and brakes.

Navigation display

In front of each pilot there is a display screen showing the aircraft's position, direction of flight, and route. The display is shown here in "compass rose" mode. Directions are shown as numbers that must be multiplied by 10 (21 means 210 degrees, etc.). The plane's autopilot is "locked on" to one ground radio beacon after another. These are called VORs (for VHF omni-directional range). Here there is a VOR at 144 degrees. The distance to a VOR is given by distance-measuring equipment (DME). Fixed points along the route are called waypoints.

Radio beam

Ground speed

Distance to beacon

Time to reach beacon

Wind direction

Windspeed

Weather radar mode

The navigation display can be switched into weather radar mode. Information from the plane's forward-pointing radar is turned into a picture of the rain or snow ahead, with colours showing where it is heaviest. This can be switched off while the screen continues to show the plane's heading, speed and course. Circular arcs ahead of the plane symbol show distances — here, for example, there is one at 20 nautical miles (37 km). A planned route can be shown as a solid line from waypoint to waypoint. An alternative route can also be shown.

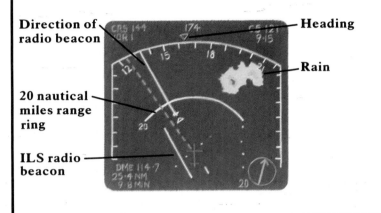

Direction of radio beacon

20 nautical miles range ring

ILS radio beacon

Heading

Rain

Primary flight display

Another screen mainly shows roll (the aircraft's tilt to left or right) and pitch (whether its nose is pointing up or down). The artificial horizon is controlled by a gyroscope which points in the same direction however much the plane rolls. To the pilot, sharing the motion of the plane, it looks as if the horizon line rolls while a bar representing the aircraft stays steady. Pointers moving along scales show height, airspeed, etc.

Airspeed scale

Horizon line

Bank angle

Height

Pitch deviation scale

Make a model artificial horizon

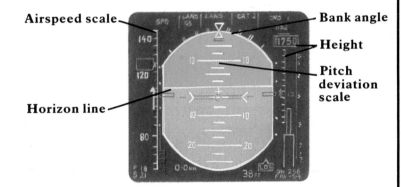

T-BAR

BASE OF POT

SHARPEN MATCH

CENTRE

SPIN GENTLY

CUT OUT TO THIS SHAPE

BEND   BEND

STICK WITH TAPE

▲ You will need a small plastic pot with a lid (one with a circular depression in its base, as shown far right, works best), a match, and a 5cm-by-8cm piece of cardboard. Cut the cardboard to the shape shown above.

▲ Take the top off the pot. Turn the pot over, and tape the T-bar to it as shown, so it stands 1.5 cm above the top. Make sure that it is level.

▲ ▶ Make a small hole in the exact centre of the lid. Push a sharpened matchstick through it, making sure it is a tight fit. This top serves as your gyro. Spin it, and you will find it stays level even if you tilt the pot.

Stand by for take-off

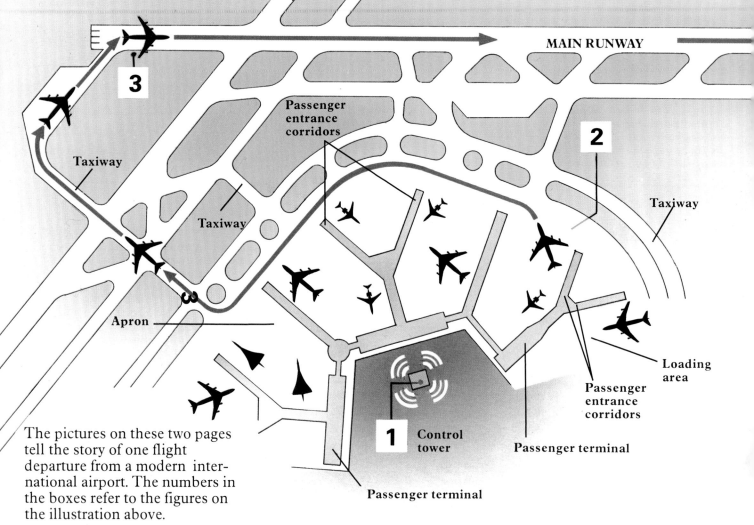

MAIN RUNWAY

3

Taxiway

Taxiway

Apron

2

Passenger entrance corridors

Taxiway

Loading area

Passenger entrance corridors

Passenger terminal

1 Control tower

Passenger terminal

The pictures on these two pages tell the story of one flight departure from a modern international airport. The numbers in the boxes refer to the figures on the illustration above.

1

▲ The most important building at any airport is the control tower. Behind windows with a clear view of all the runways, controllers pass instructions on taxiing and parking to pilots. Others control air traffic from radar screens.

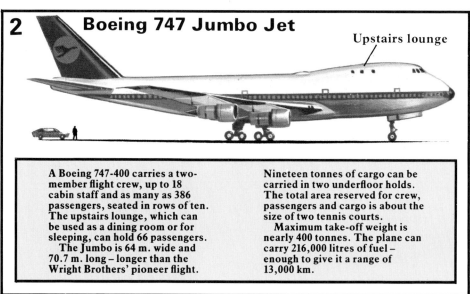

2 **Boeing 747 Jumbo Jet**

Upstairs lounge

A Boeing 747-400 carries a two-member flight crew, up to 18 cabin staff and as many as 386 passengers, seated in rows of ten. The upstairs lounge, which can be used as a dining room or for sleeping, can hold 66 passengers.
  The Jumbo is 64 m. wide and 70.7 m. long – longer than the Wright Brothers' pioneer flight.

Nineteen tonnes of cargo can be carried in two underfloor holds. The total area reserved for crew, passengers and cargo is about the size of two tennis courts.
  Maximum take-off weight is nearly 400 tonnes. The plane can carry 216,000 litres of fuel – enough to give it a range of 13,000 km.

▲ Before an aircraft can take off, the pilot has to file a flight plan and work out take-off speeds, which vary according to the plane's weight, weather conditions, runway length and the height of the airport above sea level. The plane must be fuelled, food and drink put on board, and the cargo loaded.
  The passengers get on board after clearing customs and passport control. Once they have fastened their seat-belts, the plane is ready to go.

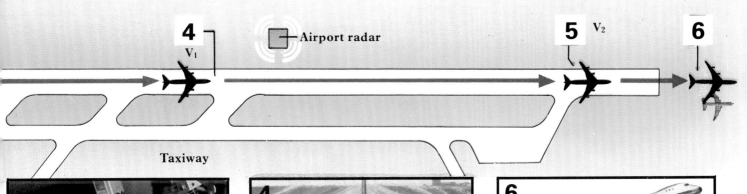

Airport radar

Taxiway

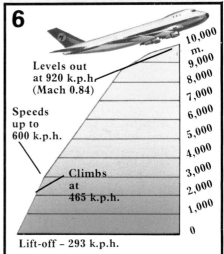

6

Levels out
at 920 k.p.h.
(Mach 0.84)

Speeds
up to
600 k.p.h.

Climbs
at
465 k.p.h.

10,000 m.
9,000
8,000
7,000
6,000
5,000
4,000
3,000
2,000
1,000
0

Lift-off – 293 k.p.h.

▲ The controllers give the pilot clearance to taxi to a holding point near the beginning of the runway. When checks have been completed, permission to take off is given. The aircraft taxis onto the runway and revs up its engines.

▲ The aircraft moves down the runway, gathering speed. Once V₁ is reached, the plane is going too fast to have room to stop. V₂ is safe flying speed. For a typical Jumbo take-off, these speeds are 265 and 293 k.p.h.

▲ As the plane climbs away from the runway it may have to throttle back to meet noise restrictions. Departure controllers guide the pilot onto the right course. On leaving the airport control area he set his course along an airway.

Keeping the engines supplied with fuel

A Jumbo Jet's four engines can gulp a total of more than 11,000 kg. of fuel every hour, but the plane is still one of the most economical forms of transport.
   A separate tank is provided for each engine, but cross-feed valves allow all tanks to feed any engine.

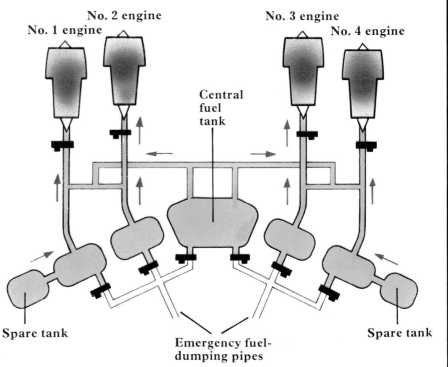

No. 2 engine
No. 1 engine
No. 3 engine
No. 4 engine

Central
fuel
tank

Spare tank

Emergency fuel-
dumping pipes

Spare tank

Fuel-hungry jet liners

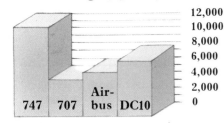

12,000
10,000
8,000
6,000
4,000
2,000
0

747 | 707 | Air-bus | DC10

This chart shows how many kg. of fuel these aircraft use every hour of flight.

Flight 593 to Perth

1 Local time (20.30) Body time (20.30)

▲ Foxtrot Tango, a Boeing 747-400, takes off for Australia from Heathrow Airport. In each panel following, the clocks show local time (left) and "body time" (right) — the time in Britain, to which the passengers' bodies are still attuned.

2 (22.30) (21.30)

▲ Mealtime. The 18-strong cabin crew heat pre-packed frozen meals in fast-working microwave ovens in the Jumbo's 14 galley areas. After the meal, passengers can watch a film or listen to a choice of taped entertainment on headphones.

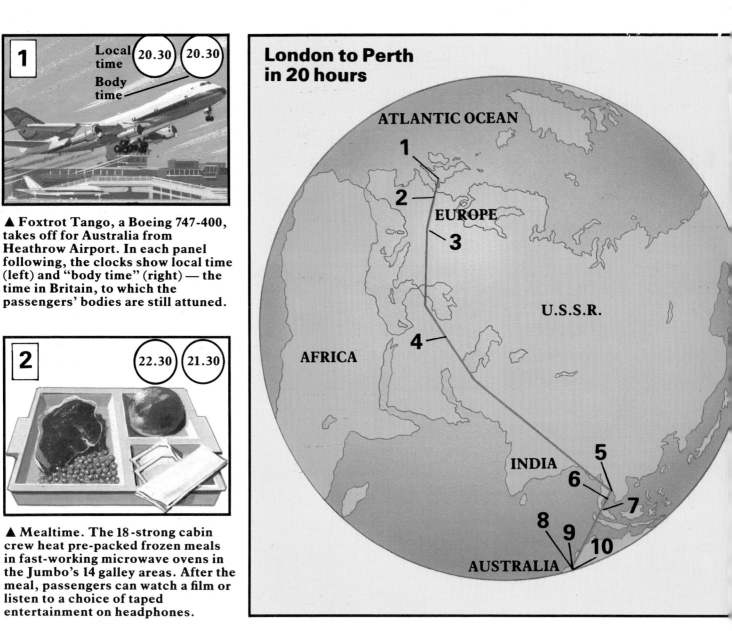

London to Perth in 20 hours

ATLANTIC OCEAN

1
2
EUROPE
3

U.S.S.R.

AFRICA

4

INDIA

5
6
7
8
9
10

AUSTRALIA

3 (23.30) (22.30)

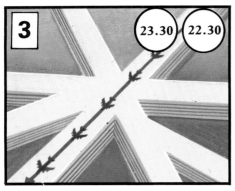

▲ The jet flies down an airway, a corridor in the sky marked out by radio signal beacons. Planes are separated by large distances horizontally and vertically. The jet is over Europe, where local time is one hour ahead of London time.

4 (02.30) (23.30)

▲ The 747 flies 12 km high through the night. The air temperature outside is -57°C. Water vapour from the jet exhausts freezes into tiny ice particles, forming condensation trails. Body time now lags 3 hours behind local time.

5 (14.25) (07.25)

▲ After nearly 11 hours' flying, Foxtrot Tango makes its first stopover, at Bangkok in Thailand. The aircraft is refuelled, and a new flight crew takes over. For safety reasons flight crews do not usually fly more than 11 hours at a time.

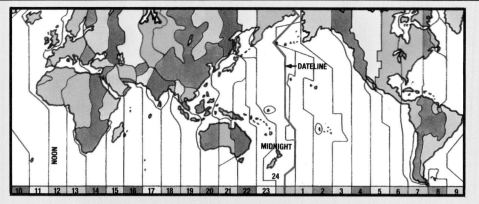

10 (00.40) (16.40)

▲ A gentle touchdown, and Flight 593 is over. The passengers disembark after 20 hours with eight hours of jet lag. What seems to them to be afternoon is midnight in Perth. If they had flown the other way, the time difference would be reversed.

▲ As the chart shows, the hour of day at any one time differs around the world. One problem of long-distance jet flights is that they pass through several time zones too quickly for people to adapt.

Passengers like those on Flight 593, who land just past midnight feeling as though it were late afternoon are said to be suffering from jet-lag.

▼ Radar equipment is used throughout the flight to check on weather conditions ahead of the plane. It can warn the pilot of thunderstorms 200 km away, and can show him whether there is a cloud cover over the airport he is heading for.

The radar weather picture is displayed on a screen in the cockpit.

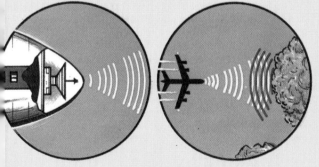

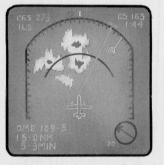

▲ Radar pulse is sent out from a dish in the plane's nose.

▲ Hitting a cloud, it bounces back towards the plane.

▲ Incoming pulses are transmitted from receiver to screen.

9 (00.25) (16.25)

▲ The pilot's instruments use radio signals from ILS (instrument landing system) transmitters near the runway as the Jumbo comes down. Indicators show how far the plane is above or below, and left or right of, the correct approach path.

6 (16.35) (09.35)

▲ After an hour the plane is on its way again. It is kept in straight and steady flight by the automatic pilot. The aircraft's position is constantly calculated by the onboard navigation system. The data is then fed to the autopilot.

7 (18.35) (10.35)

▲ Foxtrot Tango lands for a second stopover, at Kuala Lumpur in Malaysia. Flight 593 has covered over 11,000 km, and there are over 4,000 km still to go. But they are now in their destination's time zone, so jet lag will not increase.

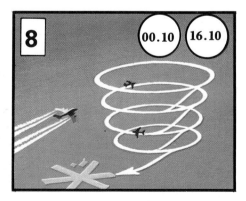

8 (00.10) (16.10)

▲ Near the end of the flight's last leg, the 747 starts to descend while more than 100 km from its destination. Some aircraft are waiting to land at Perth, so the plane is 'stacked', circling a radio beacon while waiting for clearance to land.

The sound barrier

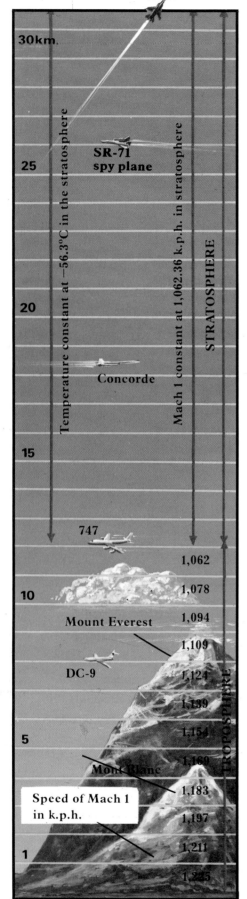

MiG-25 37 km. height record

30km.

Temperature constant at −56.3°C in the stratosphere

SR-71
spy plane

25

Mach 1 constant at 1,062.36 k.p.h. in stratosphere

STRATOSPHERE

20

Concorde

15

747 · 1,062

10 · 1,078

Mount Everest · 1,094
· 1,109
DC-9 · 1,124
· 1,139
· 1,154

5

Mont Blanc · 1,169
· 1,183
Speed of Mach 1
in k.p.h. · 1,197
· 1,211
1 · 1,225

TROPOSPHERE

Sound travels at different speeds at different levels. At sea level its speed is about 1,225 k.p.h., but it slows down in the cold air higher up.

An Austrian scientist called Ernst Mach worked out a way of comparing speed through the air directly to the speed of sound which is called Mach 1 after him. Mach 2 is exactly twice the speed of sound, and so on.

Aircraft that travel faster than sound must pass through shock waves (see below) that slow them down. These waves are what is popularly known as the sound barrier.

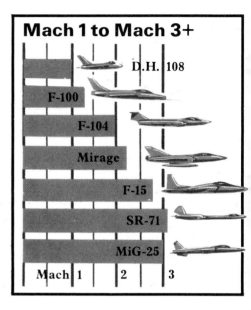

Mach 1 to Mach 3+

D.H. 108

F-100

F-104

Mirage

F-15

SR-71

MiG-25

Mach 1   2   3

Booming along on the shock cone

The illustration below shows three moments in the flight of a single jet, as it accelerates up to and beyond the speed of sound.

The nearly circular lines surrounding the aircraft (1) are the air disturbances its flight causes. They are known as pressure waves. As they move away from the plane they gradually get weaker, as

the ripples die away after a stone has been thrown into a pond. These pressure waves travel at exactly the speed of sound.

As the aircraft goes faster (2), it catches up on the pressure waves moving ahead of it. At Mach 1 it is travelling as fast as they are. It pushes all the air ripples that would previously have had

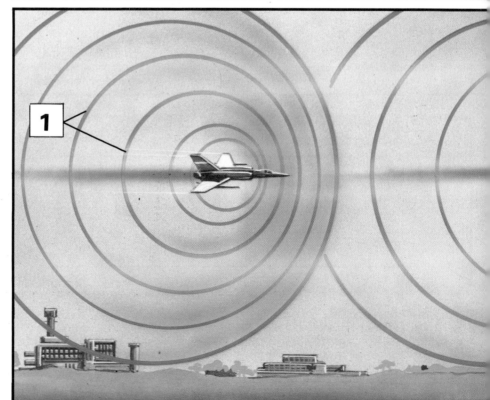

1

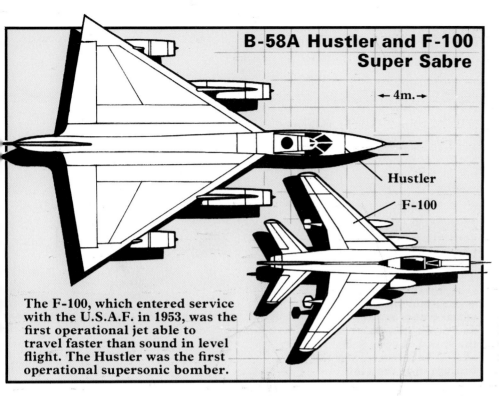

B-58A Hustler and F-100 Super Sabre

← 4m. →

Hustler

F-100

The F-100, which entered service with the U.S.A.F. in 1953, was the first operational jet able to travel faster than sound in level flight. The Hustler was the first operational supersonic bomber.

Sound power

The sonic boom is a spectacular example of sound power. Here is a small-scale sound experiment.

SUGAR

PIECE OF POLYTHENE

RUBBER BAND

▲ You will need a tin tray, an empty jar, some polythene and a little sugar. Put the polythene over the top of the jar, and fasten it with a rubber band. Smooth it down so that it is perfectly flat, and put a few grains of sugar on it.

time to spread out ahead of it into one vertical Mach wave (3).

When the plane is travelling faster than sound (4), it pushes the tip of the Mach wave with it, bending the wave into a cone shape. Where the lower edge of the cone reaches the ground, there is a sudden increase in air pressure that you can hear as a double boom, or if the shock waves are very close together as one bang.

Supersonic planes trail the sonic boom in their wake over the entire region they pass over while travelling faster than sound. The area over which it can be heard is called the plane's 'carpet'. The carpet of Concorde, for example, is nearly 90 km. wide.

▲ Hold the tin tray about 10 cm. away from the jar, and hit it with something hard. The pressure wave that you hear as a bang will have the power to make the sugar jump. In the same way the sonic boom can damage windows and buildings.

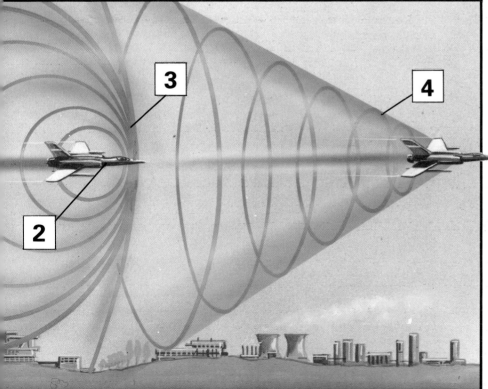

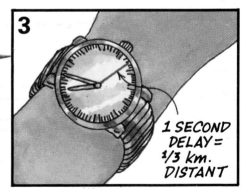

1 SECOND DELAY = ¹/₃ km. DISTANT

▲ Remembering the speed of sound can also be useful, for instance in a thunderstorm. To work out how many kilometres away it is, count the number of seconds between the lightning flash and the thunderclap and divide by 3.

Supersonic airliners

Supersonic military planes have been in service since 1953, but civilian supersonic transports (SSTs) took longer to develop.

The first SST to fly was the Russian Tupolev Tu-144, in 1968. The Anglo-French Concorde first flew two months later, and now regularly crosses the Atlantic. The Tupolev was soon withdrawn from passenger service.

The United States also laid plans for an SST in the 1960s. The project was eventually given up because of its cost, and as a result of public opposition based on fear of high noise levels and possible harm to the atmosphere.

Aircraft designers continue to work on a likely supersonic successor to Concorde. This design is for a 300-seat, trans-Pacific supersonic airliner which will travel at between two and two-and-a-half times the speed of sound. It should be in service by the beginning of the 21st century.

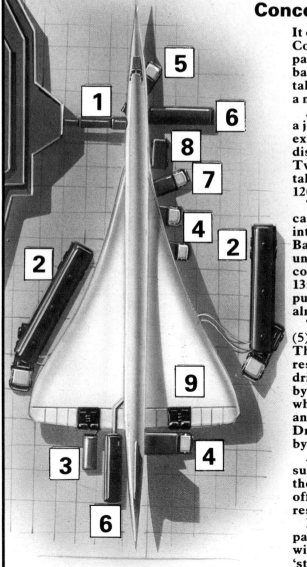

Concorde on the apron

It only takes 30 minutes for Concorde to unload its passengers and their baggage, to refuel, and to take on new provisions and a new load of passengers.

As soon as the jet stops, a jetway (1) noses up to the exit. All passengers disembark in five minutes. Two giant refuellers (2) take 18 minutes to pump in 120,000 litres of kerosene.

The air-conditioning cart (3) pumps fresh air into the passenger cabin. Baggage vehicles (4) unload the underfloor compartments at a rate of 135 kg a minute, and then put a new load aboard almost as fast.

The toilets are cleaned (5) and the drains checked. The plane's galleys are restocked with food, drinks and duty-free goods by special vehicles (6) which rise up to cabin level and 'plug in' to the doors. Drinking water is supplied by a bowser (7).

A ground power unit (8) supplies electricity while the jet's engines are shut off, and a similar truck restarts the engines (9).

By this time the new passengers are aboard with their baggage, and it's 'stand by for take off' again.

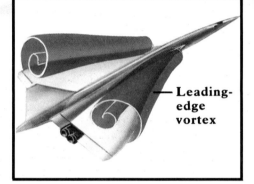

▲ The wings of the SSTs are ogival-shaped like a delta with the edges rounded off. A spiral current of air called the leading-edge vortex forms over them in flight. It stays there even at slow speeds, increasing lift.

Leading-edge vortex

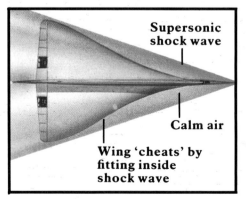

Supersonic shock wave

Calm air

Wing 'cheats' by fitting inside shock wave

▲ As Concorde rushes through the air at Mach 2, a supersonic shock wave streams back from the nose. Its wings fit inside the cone of undisturbed air behind the shock wave, giving the plane and its passengers a smooth ride.

Aircraft and noise

All aircraft are noisy, and jets are noisier than most. Noise levels, particularly around airports, have mounted as more and bigger jets have come into service. Public criticism of jet noise has also grown, and designers now spend a lot of thought on finding ways of making jets quieter.

The roar of a jet engine is produced mainly by the violent mixing of its exhaust gases with the outside air. How loud it is depends on the speed at which the gases meet the air. It is greatest when the engines are run up to full power just before the plane takes off.

One way of reducing noise is to use turbofan engines in which much of the air taken in bypasses the combustion chamber, thus reducing the exhaust speeds. Turbofans are now used in most modern jet transports.

Inside the ear

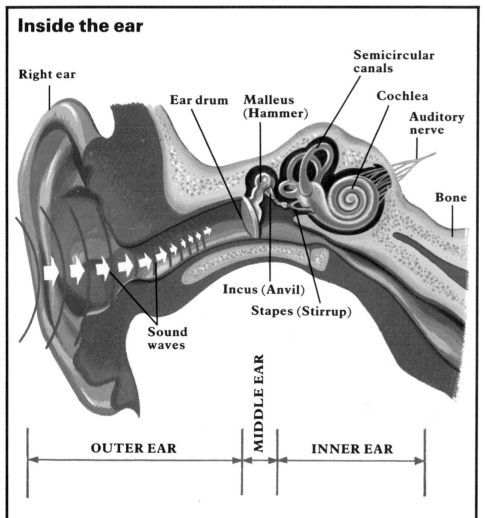

Right ear

Ear drum

Malleus (Hammer)

Semicircular canals

Cochlea

Auditory nerve

Bone

Sound waves

Incus (Anvil)

Stapes (Stirrup)

OUTER EAR | MIDDLE EAR | INNER EAR

▲ As a jet flies above you, it sends out sound waves in the form of variations in pressure in the air. The waves cause vibrations in your ear drum, which transmits them through three small bones — the hammer, anvil and stirrup — in the air-filled middle ear.

The vibrations next move into the fluid-filled inner ear, passing through the semi-circular canals (which control your balance) and the cochlea. The auditory nerve detects movements of fluid in the cochlea, and turns them into coded impulses. These pass to the brain, where the impulses are decoded and the sound is 'heard'.

Jet noise

Jet noise is usually measured in effective perceived noise decibels (EPNdB), which take into account the tone of a noise and how long it lasts as well as its loudness. The figures below are all given in EPNdB.

An increase of ten EPNdB means twice the amount of noise — so a sound that measures 60 EPNdB seems twice as noisy to the listener as one of 50 EPNdB, and so on.

Description	EPNdB
The rustling of leaves in a gentle breeze.	33
Soft whispering between 1 and 2 m away.	47
Normal speech, or the noise in a busy shop.	73
The background hum in a crowded restaurant.	78
Loud music on a record-player in a large room.	95
The roar of city traffic. A diesel lorry 8 m away.	105
A Boeing 747 taking off overhead.	107
A motor-mower cutting a lawn, or an air compressor.	112
A Boeing 707 coming in to land at an airport.	118
Concorde taking off overhead.	120

Jet fighters

Jet fighters have come a long way since Me 262s and Meteors flew in World War 2. Subsonic Sabres and MiG-15s met in the first jet combats in 1950, during the Korean War, and now air forces throughout the world are equipped with advanced supersonic fighters

The aircraft shown here date from the Korean War to the present day. Other classic fighters include the Mirage F.1C (see p. 3) and the Tornado (see p.27). All but the Sabre and the MiG-15 use after-burning jet engines and carry target-detecting radar equipment.

The dates give the year of each plane's entry into service.

North American F-86 Sabre 1949

◄ The North American F-86 Sabre was the second American plane to break the sound barrier, and at one time held the world air speed record at 1,073 kph. It really made its mark in the Korean War, in which a total of 792 MiG-15s fell victim to its six 12.7 mm machine-guns and rockets.

◄ Russia's MiG-15, flown by Chinese pilots, was more than a match for early American jet fighters over Korea, being 100 kph faster than the U.S.A.F.'s F-80C Shooting Star and the U.S. Navy's F9F Panther. But it did not always win, and in its first week of use one was shot down to become the first victim of an all-jet combat.

Mikoyan MiG-15 1948

SEPECAT Jaguar GR.1A 1972

▲ This Anglo-French strike aircraft was first designed as a trainer and light attack aircraft. Its maximum speed is Mach 1.6, and it is very agile. It carries advanced electronics and can take off from rough airstrips with heavy weapons loads.

Lockheed F-104 Starfighter 1958

► The Starfighter has been nick-named 'the missile with a man in it' because of its slim, needle-nosed shape and small wings. The wings are so sharp that the leading edges have to be covered to protect ground workers from cutting themselves.

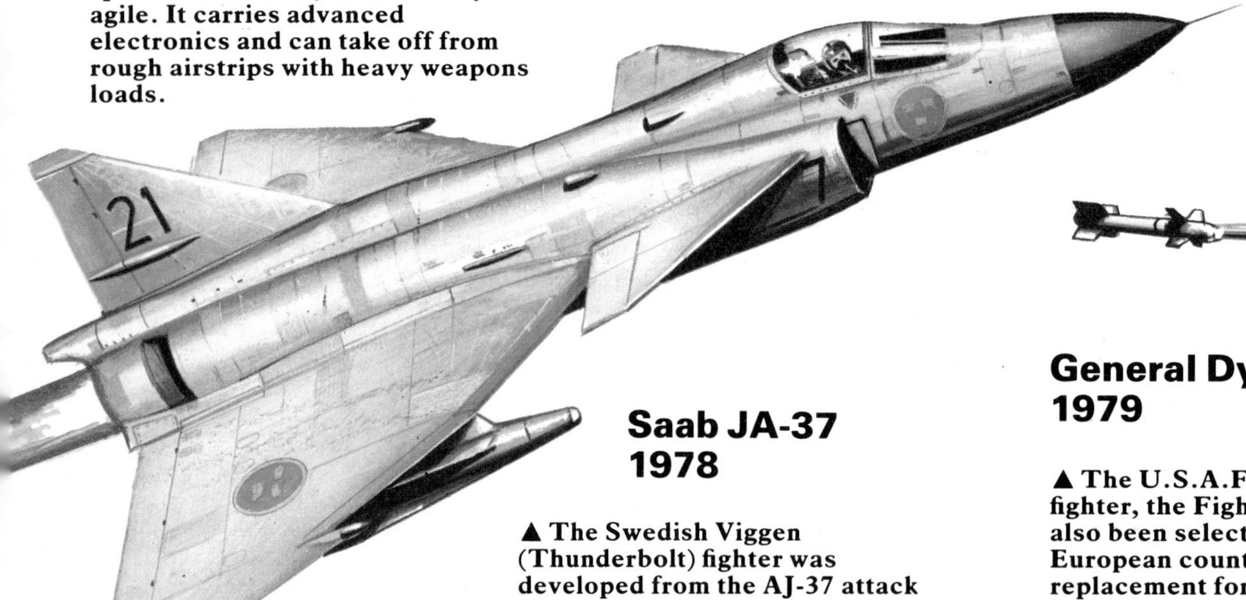

Saab JA-37 1978

▲ The Swedish Viggen (Thunderbolt) fighter was developed from the AJ-37 attack version. The JA-37 carries guns in a pack mounted under the plane's belly. Like the earlier versions it can operate from ordinary roads as well as airfields.

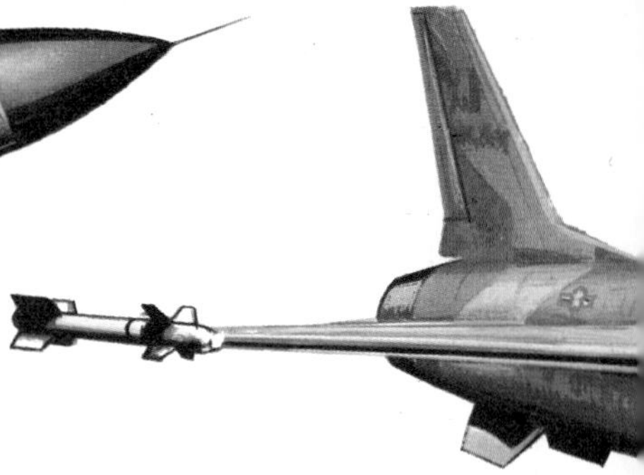

General Dynamics F-16 1979

▲ The U.S.A.F.'s air combat fighter, the Fighting Falcon, has also been selected by several European countries as a replacement for their Starfighters. It is one of the most manoeuvrable fighters ever built. There is a slightly lower-powered version which is known as the F16/79.

B.A.C. Lightning 1960

Detachable fuel tank

McDonnell Douglas F-4 Phantom II 1960

▲ The Phantom is one of the world's most widely used advanced warplanes. It was developed because the U.S. Navy needed a twin-engined fighter to operate from aircraft carriers. Although no longer produced, well over 2,000 are still in service and are constantly updated.

The Phantom has a large radar for air combat and is armed with air-to-air missiles and a built-in six-barrelled cannon. It can also be used for ground attack with bombs, missiles and the cannon.

McDonnell Douglas F-18 Hornet 1982

▲ The Lightning was the first supersonic plane to enter service with the R.A.F. It can accelerate from Mach 1 to Mach 2 in 3½ minutes.

The Lightning was outstanding as a high-level interceptor, being able to climb almost vertically, straight after take-off. At least one unsuspecting U-2 spy plane flying at 25,000 m has been pounced on by a Lightning.

► The Hornet is mainly flown from carriers by the U.S. Marine Corps, as either an interceptor or a ground attack aircraft. The plane can reach Mach 1.8 at high altitude.

Mikoyan MiG-23 1972

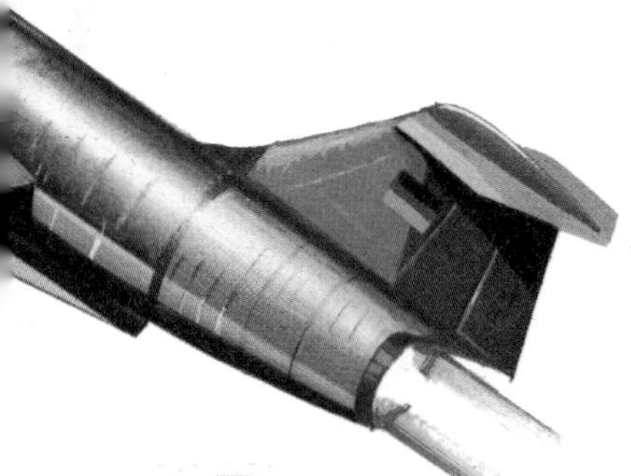

► Russia's swing-winged MiG-23 fighter-bomber flies from bases in Eastern Europe, and has also been supplied to Middle-East countries. The all-weather fighter version has a large nose to house radar equipment. There are also ground-attack and two-seat trainer versions.

Grumman F-14 Tomcat 1974

► The Tomcat is in service on the U.S. Navy's aircraft carriers. Its main purpose is fleet defence and tactical air support. An additional role is photographic reconnaissance. Its radar can detect targets 250 km away and can track up to 24 objects at the same time.

23

Bombers and strike aircraft

Until the 1960s bombers were designed to approach their targets at great height, making their final bombing runs in straight lines for the greatest accuracy. They were often unarmed, though the B-52 carried a tail gun. Then anti-aircraft defence relying on radar was improved. Now 'strike' aircraft are designed to fly low as well as fast to their targets, closely following ground contours, ducking under enemy radar, and taking advantage of radar-blocking obstacles such as hills. ECM (electronic counter-measures) equipment detects enemy radar and automatically sends back confusing signals of its own. The plane scatters radar-reflection foil ('chaff') and decoy flares that lure away incoming missiles. No human pilot could handle all this, so the aircraft is largely computer-controlled.

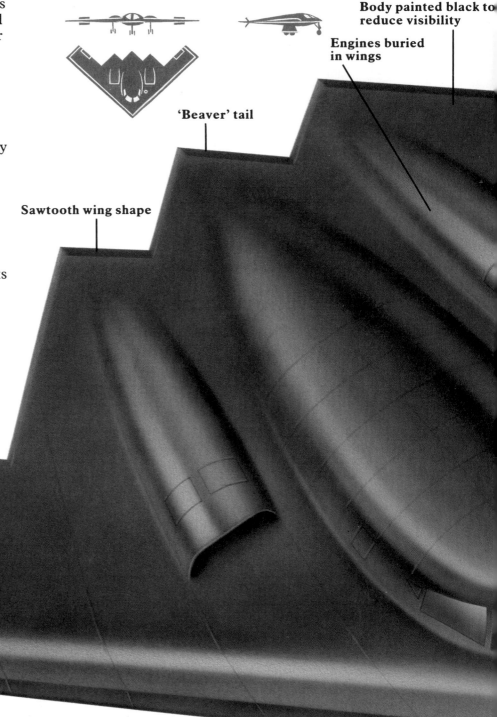

Sawtooth wing shape

'Beaver' tail

Body painted black to reduce visibility

Engines buried in wings

British Aerospace Buccaneer S.2 1963

▲ When Britain abandoned its conventional aircraft carriers, this fast and powerful strike aircraft, originally intended for naval use, was assigned to the RAF. It can carry four bombs in its weapons bay and four missiles under its wings. Because it is economical on fuel and can be refuelled in flight through the probe in front of the cockpit, it has a typical range of 3,700 km.

Fairchild Republic A-10A Thunderbolt II 1975

► The lumbering 'Warthog' is a tank-killing machine, able to use short, rough battlefield airstrips. It can fly at no more than 680 km per hour, but it is heavily armoured against ground fire. Its nose gun can fire 70 rounds a second — each the size of a milk bottle.

Boeing B-52 Stratofortress 1955

▲ The eight-engined B-52 is the world's heaviest bomber, weighing over 200 tonnes on take-off. It is 48 m long, has a wingspan of over 56 m and can travel at 1,050 km per hour. It carries nuclear-tipped cruise missiles or conventional free-fall bombs.

Rockwell International B-1B 1986

► This advanced supersonic nuclear bomber has slender lines and variable-geometry 'swing wings', which are swept back for high-speed flight, and extended at other times. Afterburners on the four turbofan engines give the plane a maximum speed of Mach 2.

Rounded cabin

Northrop B-2 Stealth bomber 1989

▲ The Stealth bomber's strange 'flying wing' shape is designed to reduce radar reflections, and the plane is made of special radar-absorbent materials. It was first used in combat during the Gulf War.

Spies in the sky

High-flying jets regularly keep watch on other countries' military activity. The American U-2 spy plane had long wings that gave it a lot of lift, even in the thin air at high altitudes, and it could glide for long distances to save fuel.

The MiG-25 Foxbat flies at about 27 km at Mach 3.2. It carries SLAR (sideways-looking airborne radar) and has five cameras in its nose.

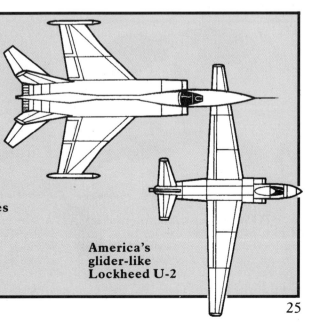

America's glider-like Lockheed U-2

25

Jump-jets and swing-wings

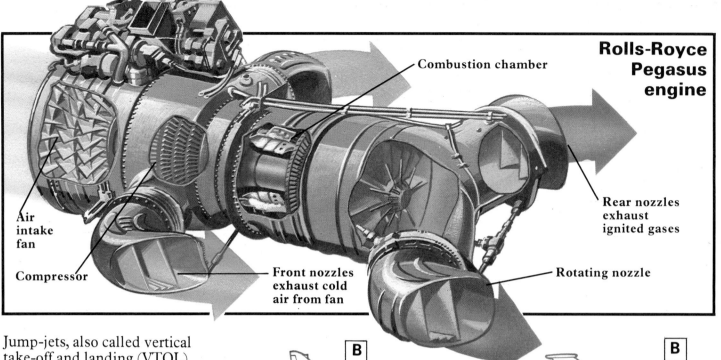

Rolls-Royce Pegasus engine

Combustion chamber

Rear nozzles exhaust ignited gases

Air intake fan

Compressor

Front nozzles exhaust cold air from fan

Rotating nozzle

Jump-jets, also called vertical take-off and landing (VTOL) planes, do not need runways. This means that military jump-jets are not put out of action if their airfield is bombed. They can also operate from decks of small ships without using catapults and arrester wires.

Early work on VTOL was done with the 'Flying Bedstead' (see page 30), and experimental VTOL craft have been built in America, Russia, France and Germany. The Hawker Siddeley Harrier, powered by the Pegasus engine shown above, was the first jump-jet to enter service, in 1969.

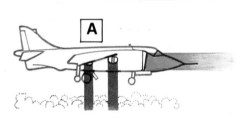

▲ The four exhaust nozzles of the Harrier's Pegasus engine point vertically down for take-off (A). They gradually swivel back until the plane is flying fast enough for its wings to keep it in the air (B). The process is reversed for landing.

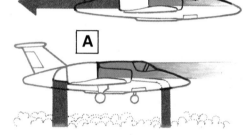

▲ The projected McDonnell Douglas 260 had three fans, one in the nose and the other two above the wings. The company has since concentrated on an advanced version of the Harrier for the U.S. Marine Corps.

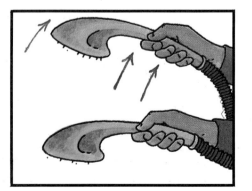

▲ VTO works just like normal jet flight, except that the jet is deflected downwards and so forces the aircraft up. Try holding a hand-shower over the bath, and turning it on fast. The force of the water gushing out will push your hand up.

1 Faster enemy jet closing in to attack

Harrier pilot turns his jet nozzles to forward position

▲ The jump-jet is at an advantage in air-to-air combat. If a Harrier is being chased by another fighter it can escape by a technique called V.I.F.F. (Vectoring In Forward Flight). The pilot swivels the nozzles from the fully back position

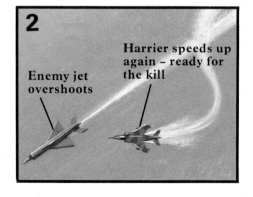

2 Harrier speeds up again – ready for the kill

Enemy jet overshoots

to as far forward as they will go. Its jets now slow the Harrier down much faster than air brakes can, so the pursuing fighter flies past. The Harrier pilot can then turn the nozzles back and get on the tail of the other plane.

Tri-national swing-wing – the Panavia Tornado

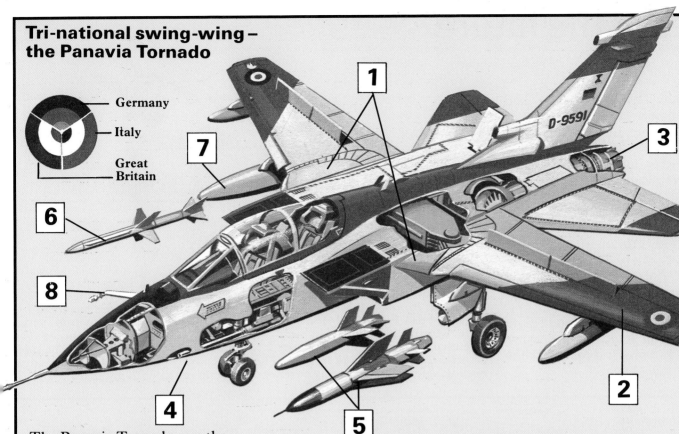

Germany
Italy
Great Britain

The Panavia Tornado was the first European swing-wing to enter service. Training began in 1981 with aircraft equipping squadrons in 1982. The first swing-wing plane in military service was the General Dynamics F-111.

By using moving or 'variable geometry' wings, the Tornado combines the advantages of long straight wings for slow flying and landing with a fully swept layout for high-speed.

The part of the wing near the fuselage (1) is fixed, while the outer section (2) can swing backwards or forwards. The two RB 199 turbofan engines exhaust through thrust-reversing buckets (3) to shorten the landing run.

Weapons include two built-in 27 mm cannon (4), various air-to-surface missiles (5), and air-to-air missiles like the Sparrow (6). Fuel can be carried in tanks under the wings (7) as well as internally. There is also a probe (8) for in-flight fuelling.

▶The Tornado's pilot can vary the sweepback of his wings. Straight for take-off and landing, swept-back for high speed flight. The swing-wings are connected to a rigid box in the fuselage, and are moved by hydraulic jacks.

Wing sweeps through this angle

Pilot to scale

▲ The pioneer of swing-wing flight was the Bell X-5 research aircraft of 1951. It was based on Messerschmitt designs that came into American hands at the end of World War 2. Its success led, in 1953, to the development of the Grumman Jaguar, a carrier-borne fighter, but the project was abandoned after two prototypes had been completed.

Jets of the future

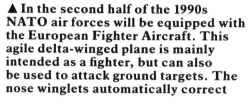

Tomorrow's jets will go faster and higher than today's, yet travel farther for each litre of fuel, and be quieter. They may one day be fuelled by liquid hydrogen, which would be non-polluting and plentiful, but would need to be refrigerated and would require huge fuel tanks.

A new generation of supersonic airliner, flying to Mach 3, may be built. Following these may come the spaceplane, propelled by a hybrid engine: it would be a fanjet, for take-off and low-altitude flight then a ramjet at altitude (see panel below), and finally a rocket, when at the fringe of space.

▲ In the second half of the 1990s NATO air forces will be equipped with the European Fighter Aircraft. This agile delta-winged plane is mainly intended as a fighter, but can also be used to attack ground targets. The nose winglets automatically correct the plane's flight as it is buffeted by turbulent air at high speed and low altitude. The EFA would instantl crash if it were not flown moment to moment by its computers. The pilot will control some functions by spoken commands.

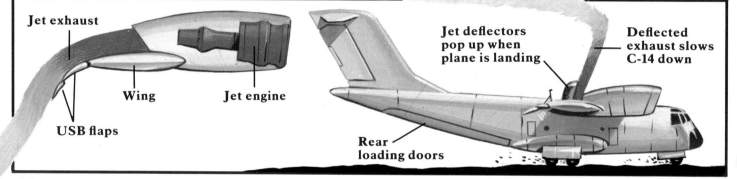

Jet exhaust

Wing

Jet engine

USB flaps

Jet deflectors pop up when plane is landing

Deflected exhaust slows C-14 down

Rear loading doors

▲ A system called U.S.B. (upper surface blowing) makes planes capable of short take-offs and landings. The engines are mounted over the wings, as in the pioneering Boeing C-14.

U.S.B. works like this: Jet exhaust gases blow over the wing's upper surface. U.S.B. flaps curve down behind the wing's trailing edge, pointing towards the ground. The exhaust gases stick to the flaps and are deflected almost straight downwards, creating lift.

You can see what happens by holding the back of a spoon against the water from a tap. The gases stick to the flaps just as the water curves around the spoon. The effect is now put to work in some airliners — the Soviet An-72 and An-74, and the Japanese Asuka.

Hypersonic ramjets

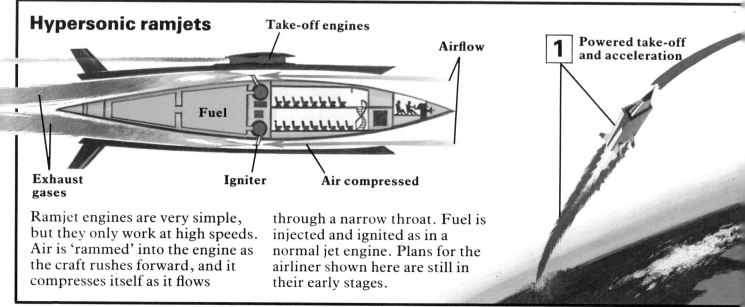

Take-off engines

Airflow

Fuel

Exhaust gases

Igniter

Air compressed

1 Powered take-off and acceleration

Ramjet engines are very simple, but they only work at high speeds. Air is 'rammed' into the engine as the craft rushes forward, and it compresses itself as it flows through a narrow throat. Fuel is injected and ignited as in a normal jet engine. Plans for the airliner shown here are still in their early stages.

Jet airliners may be growing propellers in the next few years. The unducted fan — also known as a propfan or ultra-high-bypass engine — is the latest development of the jet engine. Like a fanjet, (see page 7), it consists of a turbojet with a built-in fan, or propeller, either at the front or the back, which gives extra thrust. It differs from a fanjet in that a higher proportion of the intake air bypasses the turbojet core. The fan is mounted on the same axle as the turbine in the engine, which is rotated by the expansion of the hot exhaust gases.

A propfan engine is quiet and economical by comparison with a turbojet or fanjet of equivalent power. In fact the fuel costs over a 650-km journey of the McDonnell Douglas MD-80 testbed plane, shown here, could be half those of the company's comparable DC-9.

The blades of a propfan may be unducted — that is, exposed as here (right) — or ducted — placed inside a tube that gives greater protection from damage and also reduces the damage caused if a fan should break off.

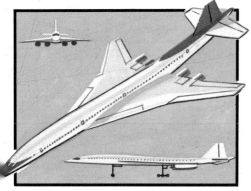

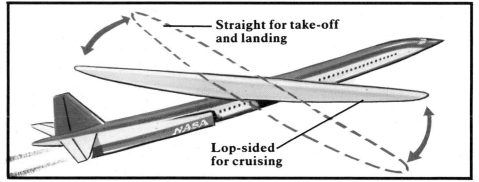

Straight for take-off and landing

Lop-sided for cruising

▲ This McDonnell Douglas design for a supersonic liner would carry 273 passengers at Mach 2.2. It has unusually shaped wings intended to cause less drag than ogival wings of the type used on Concorde.

▲ The weird, scissor-like swing-wing aircraft above is a design study by NASA. It would be an easy and lightweight way to give jet airliners swing-wings, because the design only calls for one swivel point — the heaviest part of any swing-wing aircraft. The four turbofan engines are mounted in long ducts on the tail.

The idea is not new. German designers drew up similar plans in World War 2, for a fighter to be called the Blohm und Voss P 202.

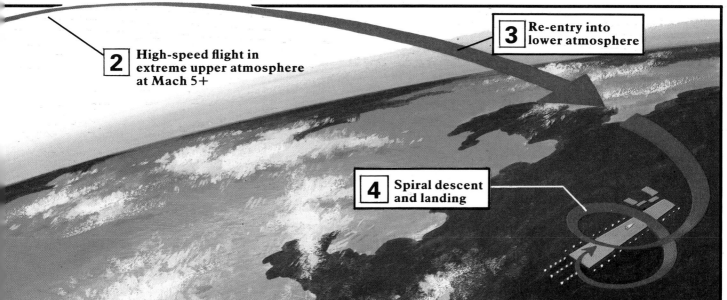

2 High-speed flight in extreme upper atmosphere at Mach 5+

3 Re-entry into lower atmosphere

4 Spiral descent and landing

Jet firsts

The first man to suggest jet air travel was the French balloonist Joseph Montgolfier. In 1783 he proposed (but did not succeed in) using the hot air that kept his balloons up to drive them forward. Here are some later pioneers from jet flight's short but crowded history.

Flying Bedstead

1865
First real design for a jet-propelled plane drawn up by de Louvrié, a French engineer.

1865's jet

August 27, 1939
Capt. Erich Warsitz made the first jet flight, in a Heinkel He 178 test plane.

November 30, 1941
First cross-country jet flight, made in the Italian Caproni-Campini N-1 from Milan to Rome.

July 27, 1944
Gloster Meteors of the RAF made first jet combat flight, against V-1 flying bombs.

September 18, 1948
The Convair XF-92A research aircraft was the first delta-wing jet to fly.

July 27, 1949
The de Havilland Comet was the first pure-jet airliner to fly. It went into service in 1952.

November 8, 1950
First jet-vs.-jet air victory won by a Lockheed F-80 over a Chinese MiG-15 in Korean War.

August 3, 1954
First VTO jet flight, made by Rolls-Royce test pilot R.T. Shepherd in the 'Flying Bedstead'.

October 1959
First round-the-world jet passenger service started by Pan American, using Boeing 707s.

December 31, 1968
Russia's Tupolev Tu-144 made its maiden flight, becoming the first SST to fly.

April 1, 1969
Hawker Siddeley Harriers of the RAF became the first operational VTOL aircraft.

January 22, 1970
First Boeing 747 'Jumbo Jet' entered service on Pan Am's New York – London route.

January 21, 1976
Concorde made the first SST passenger flights. The Tu-144 had made mail flights earlier.

April, 1988
Airbus A320 enters service with the most advanced electronics of any airliner to date.

July 17, 1989
Northrop B-2 Stealth bomber, designed to be 'low observable' by radar, makes first flight.

Abbreviations

BAe	British Aerospace	**RAF**	(British) Royal Air Force
EPNdB	Effective Perceived Noise Decibels	**SLAR**	Sideways-Looking Airborne Radar
ECM	Electronic Countermeasures	**SST**	Supersonic Transport
Flt. Lt.	Flight Lieutenant	**STOL**	Short Take-Off and Landing
ILS	Instrument Landing System	**USAF**	United States Air Force
NASA	National Aeronautics and Space Administration	**VTOL**	Vertical Take-Off and Landing

Jet facts

Did you know that jet fighters can fly faster than the shells they fire, and that at least one jet has shot itself down? These are some other odd facts about jets and the men who fly them.

America's E-3A AWACS (Airborne Warning and Control System) is a flying command base, carrying 'look down' radar that can survey a battlefield from a safe distance. Each one costs $178 million, making it one of the world's most expensive planes.

The longest scheduled non-stop flight is from Brussels to Hawaii, a distance of 11,791 km., which takes 14 hours in a Boeing 747.

A modified MiG-25 Foxbat fighter has reached a height of 37.65 km., the world absolute altitude record. It can reach a height of 35 km. in 4 mins. 11.3 secs., at a climbing speed of 400 m. a second (well over Mach 1).

On December 20, 1968, United Air Lines carried 118,519 passengers in one day in its all-jet fleet of airliners.

Leduc 0.10 ramjet

Languedoc carrier aircraft

Three prototype ramjets called Leduc 0.10s were built and successfully tested in France, making their first powered flight in 1949. They were air-launched from larger planes, and reached speeds of up to 800 k.p.h. on half-power. A later French research plane, the Nord Griffon, used a turbo-jet engine in the centre of a huge ramjet to provide power for take-off and climbing. The ramjet took over when the plane was flying high and fast.

Dornier Do31

One of the most interesting VTOL experimental aircraft was the Dornier Do31E military transport. It was powered by ten engines, with a Pegasus turbofan on each side of its fuselage and four lift-jets in removable pods on each wing-tip, and had a cruising speed of 650 k.p.h. The project was finally abandoned because of its cost and complexity.

The B-58 Hustler carried a giant-sized streamlined pod underneath its fuselage. This had two parts. The lower one was a fuel tank that could be dropped in flight once the fuel was used up. The upper part carried both fuel and a bomb or missile. This was dropped over the target zone, so that the Hustler could fly home faster and lighter.

The highest point from which airmen have made an emergency escape is 17,000 m. – nearly twice as high as Mt. Everest. On April 9, 1958, two crew members of an English Electric Canberra bomber that exploded at this height escaped unharmed. They fell 14,000 m. before their parachutes opened automatically.

The fastest jet flying-boat ever built was the Martin Seamaster, which could fly at nearly 1,000 k.p.h. Its four engines were mounted in pairs above the swept-back wings.

On December 29, 1974, a record 674 people were squeezed into a QANTAS airlines jumbo. They were being evacuated from disaster in Darwin, Australia after the town had been hit by a hurricane.

Jet words

The glossary only includes words that are not fully explained anywhere else in the book. You will find other engine words explained on pages 6 and 7, and flight words on pages 8 and 9.

Afterburning
A boosting system (also called reheat) in which fuel is injected and ignited in the jet exhaust to give extra thrust.

Dassault/Breguet
Dornier
Alpha-jet

Air brakes

Air brakes
Controls that increase drag, and so slow aircraft down.

Apron
Open space at an airport on which aircraft are parked for loading, refuelling etc.

Bowser
A tanker truck used for refuelling aircraft.

Console
An aircraft instrument panel.

Flight deck
An airliner's crew compartment.

Galley
Space for cooking food on board an airliner.

Glidepath
The path an aircraft follows as it comes in to land.

Interceptor
A fast, light warplane designed for cutting attacking aircraft or missiles off.

Jet core
The central part of the jet engine, made up of the compressor and fuel injection and ignition systems.

Leading edge
The front edge of the wing.

Operational
In service – the opposite of experimental.

Pallet
A platform for carrying cargo, with openings to fit the prongs of a fork-lift truck.

Prototype
The first model (or models) of a new make of aeroplane.

Radome
A protective covering for radar equipment.

Sensor
Any reconnaissance instrument that gathers information.

Skin temperature
The temperature on the outside of a plane.

Spoilers
Long metal plates that can be raised to disturb the airflow over wings, reducing lift.

Stacking
An air traffic control system by which aircraft approaching a busy airport are left circling a radio beacon at gradually descending levels until they are cleared to land.

Subsonic
Slower than Mach 1. Speeds between Mach 1 and Mach 5 are supersonic. Hypersonic means faster than Mach 5.

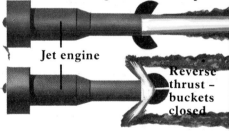

Forward flight – buckets open

Jet engine

Reverse thrust – buckets closed

Thrust-reversing buckets
Controls in the rear of a jet engine. They deflect the jet exhaust forwards, slowing the plane down.

Trailing edge
The rear edge of a wing.

Turbine
In jet engines, a wheel with curved blades that is turned by exhaust gases and itself turns the compressor.

Index